The Wizard
of Oz

by
L. Frank Baum

Adapted by
Amber D. Smith

Illustrated by
Thomas Sperling

Modern Publishing
A Division of Unisystems, Inc.
New York, New York 10022

Series UPC: 39340

Cover art by Carole Gray

This edition published by Modern Publishing,
a division of Unisystems, Inc.

Printed in Italy

Contents

Chapter 1
The Cyclone

Dorothy was a little girl who lived with her Aunt Em and Uncle Henry on a farm on the wide-open prairie in Kansas. Their home was a tiny, one-room house just big enough for two beds, a rusty old stove, a kitchen table, and a few chairs. In the middle of the floor was a trapdoor, and under that was the cellar—a safe place to hide if a cyclone came along. It was a hole dug into the ground, just big enough for the family to squeeze into.

The house sat in the midst of the great prairie. Not a tree or house broke the broad sweep of flat land that reached to the edge of the sky in every direction. The sun had baked the plowed land into a gray mass, with little cracks running through it. Even the grass was gray instead of green, for the sun had burned the long blades until they were the same color as the rest of the land.

Dorothy was often lonely. Her Aunt Em and Uncle Henry loved her very much, but they didn't laugh or play because they worked so hard on the farm. Her only playmate was her dog, Toto. He was small and black, with long, silky hair—the only thing that wasn't gray from prairie dust. Toto made Dorothy laugh, and she loved him more than anything else in the whole world.

One hot summer day, Dorothy was standing on the front porch with Uncle Henry. She watched him look anxiously at the sky, which was even grayer and gloomier than usual. From the far north, they could hear a low wail of the wind, and could see the long, gray grass bowing like waves before an approaching storm. Then, from the south, came a sharp whistling in the air. They looked that way, and saw even wilder ripples in the grass.

Suddenly, Uncle Henry stood up. "There's a cyclone coming, Em!" he yelled to his wife, who was in the house. "Get down in the cellar, and take Dorothy and Toto. I'll look after the cows."

He ran into the wind, which was now strong enough to snatch his hat off of his head and send it flying into the sky. Aunt Em ran to a window; one glance told her that danger was coming very swiftly. Frantically, she opened the trapdoor to the cellar. "Quick, Dorothy," she called as she climbed down into the hole, "get down in the cellar."

Dorothy was frightened and did as she was told. Just as she got to the trapdoor, though, Toto jumped out of her arms and ran to hide beneath her bed. "Toto, come back!" she called, running after the dog. She got down on her hands and knees and reached for him. She had just gotten a hold of him and started to stand up when there came a great shriek from the wind. The house shook so hard that she lost her footing and was thrown to the floor.

Then a strange thing happened.

The house shook and shook until it was lifted from its foundation. It whirled around two or three times and rose slowly through the air. Dorothy felt as if she were

going up in a hot-air balloon. Fortunately, the house was in the exact center of the cyclone, where the air is very calm. Nothing flew into the house, but the winds around it were so strong that they made the house climb higher and higher into the gray, stormy sky.

It was very dark and the wind howled horribly, but Dorothy found that she was riding it out quite easily. Toto, however, was frightened. He ran around barking loudly and almost fell through the open trapdoor, so Dorothy crawled over and slammed it shut.

Hour after hour passed by and, slowly, Dorothy got over her fright. She crawled across the swaying floor to her bed and lay down upon it; Toto jumped up to lie beside her.

Despite the swaying of the house and the wailing of the wind, Dorothy closed her eyes and fell fast asleep.

Chapter 2

The Munchkins

The house crashed to the ground with a sudden thump, waking Dorothy and Toto and tossing them off the bed. Confused, Dorothy stood up and rubbed her eyes. The house seemed to be in good shape, and the storm was over. Sunshine streamed through the windows and flooded the room. Dorothy ran to the door and threw it open.

She gave a cry of amazement at what she saw. The cyclone had set the house down in a beautiful countryside. Dorothy stared at the array of colors around her. She had never seen anything like this place in her entire life. There were lawns of bright green grass and trees bursting with colorful fruit. Gorgeous flowers were everywhere, and birds sang and fluttered in the trees and bushes. Nearby, a small brook was running between green banks.

Everything seemed very peaceful, and very different from Kansas.

As Dorothy gazed in wonder at her new surroundings, she noticed a group of people walking toward her. They were the oddest-looking bunch she had ever seen. They were not as big as the grown-ups she was used to, but they were not very small, either. In fact, they were about as tall as Dorothy, although, so far as looks go, they were many years older.

The three men and one woman were oddly dressed. They wore cone-shaped hats that rose a foot above their heads, with little bells around the brim that tinkled sweetly as they moved. The men's hats were blue; the woman's was white. The men, Dorothy thought, were about as old as Uncle Henry, for two of them had beards. But the woman was clearly much older. Her face was covered with wrinkles, her hair was nearly white, and she walked rather stiffly.

The little people drew near the house

where Dorothy was standing, then paused and whispered among themselves. They seemed afraid to go any closer.

Then the little old woman walked up to Dorothy, made a low bow and said, in a sweet voice, "Welcome to the land of the Munchkins, most noble Sorceress. We want to thank you for killing the Wicked Witch of the East and setting our people free from her evil control."

Dorothy listened to this speech with wonder. What could this little woman possibly mean? "You must be mistaken," Dorothy protested. "I am just a girl

from Kansas who is lost! My house blew away during a cyclone. I have not killed anything."

"Well, your house certainly did," said the woman, laughing. "See, there are her feet, still sticking out from under it!" She pointed to the corner of the house.

Dorothy looked, and gave a little cry of fright. There, indeed, just under a corner of the great beam the house rested on, were two feet, wearing silver shoes with pointed toes.

"Oh, dear!" Dorothy exclaimed. "I never meant to hurt anyone! Who was she?"

"The Wicked Witch of the East, as I said," the little woman replied. "She has held all the Munchkins in bondage for many years, making them slave for her night and day. Now they are free, and they are grateful to you for the favor."

"Are you a Munchkin?" asked Dorothy.

"No," said the little woman. "The Munchkins are the people who live here, in the East of Oz. I am the Good Witch of the North."

"Are you a real witch?" asked Dorothy, suddenly frightened. "I thought all witches were evil."

"Oh, I am certainly a real witch, but not all witches are evil. There are four witches in the land of Oz. Two—in the north and the south—are good witches, and people love us. The other two—in the east and the west—are evil witches who are feared and hated. But now, *that* is all that is left of the Wicked Witch of the East," she said, pointing once again to the feet under the house.

Just as she did this, the feet shriveled up and disappeared, leaving the sparkling, silver shoes behind. "She was so old and evil," said the Good Witch, laughing, "that she just dried up in the sun. The silver slippers are yours now. There is a charm connected with them; but what it does, we do not know."

"Thank you very much for all of your kindness," Dorothy replied as she took the silver shoes, "but can you help me find my way back to Kansas?"

The Munchkins and the Good Witch looked at each other and shrugged. They had never heard of Kansas, nor did they know how to get there. They explained that Oz was surrounded by a huge desert that no one had ever crossed.

Dorothy began to sob at this, for she felt lonely among all these strange people. Her tears saddened the kind-hearted Munchkins, and they immediately took out their handkerchiefs and began to weep with her. As for the Good Witch, she took off her cap and balanced the point on the end of her nose, while she counted to three. At once, the cap changed to a slate, on which was written in big, white chalk marks:

Let Dorothy Go to the
City of Emeralds

"There is your answer, my child," she said. "The City of Emeralds is home to Oz, a great and powerful wizard. The road to the city is paved with yellow bricks, so you cannot miss it. When you get to Oz, do not be afraid of him, but tell your story and ask him to help you."

At this, the Good Witch gave Dorothy a kiss on her forehead, which left a mark that the witch said would protect her from harm. Then the Good Witch disappeared and the Munchkins went away, leaving Dorothy and Toto all alone.

Dorothy sat down on the front porch of her house to think. She decided that she

Let Dorothy Go to the City of Emeralds

would go to Oz—otherwise, she might never see Aunt Em or Uncle Henry again. So she packed a little basket with food from her house. She washed her face, changed into a clean, blue-and-white checked dress, and put on her new silver shoes.

There were several roads nearby, but it did not take her long to find the one paved with yellow bricks. Within a short time, she was walking briskly toward the Emerald City, her silver shoes tinkling merrily along the road.

Chapter 3

The Journey Begins

Dorothy walked for hours until it started to get dark. Wondering where she might spend the evening, she stopped at a big, brightly lit blue house filled with Munchkins, all dressed in blue. Dorothy had noticed that blue seemed to be the official color of the land of the Munchkins. They were dancing and celebrating their new freedom from the Wicked Witch's evil grasp. Like every Munchkin she had passed that day, the Munchkins at the

house bowed and thanked her for killing the Wicked Witch of the East. They invited her to stay for the night, and she agreed. She ate a delicious meal and slept in a wonderfully soft bed.

The next morning at breakfast, Dorothy asked Boq, her Munchkin host, how far it was to the Emerald City.

"I do not know," he replied. "I have never been there. We Munchkins tend to keep away from Oz. I do know that it is a long way to the Emerald City—it will take you many days. The country here is rich and pleasant, but you must pass through rough and dangerous places before you reach the end of your journey."

This was not at all encouraging to Dorothy, but she was determined to get home. After finishing her meal and thanking her host, she and Toto continued along the road of yellow bricks.

When they had gone several miles, she needed to rest, so she climbed a fence and sat on its top rail. Beyond the fence was a big cornfield, and not far away was a scarecrow, placed high on a pole to keep birds from eating the ripe corn.

Dorothy leaned her chin upon her hand and gazed thoughtfully at the Scarecrow. His head was a small sack stuffed with straw, with eyes, a nose, and a mouth painted on it to represent a face. An old, pointed, blue hat was perched on his head, and the rest of the figure was a blue suit of clothes, worn and faded, which had also been stuffed with straw.

While Dorothy was gazing at the Scarecrow's painted face, she was surprised to see one of his eyes slowly wink at her.

"Good afternoon," said the Scarecrow, in a rather husky voice.

Dorothy, in complete amazement, said cautiously, "Did you say something?"

"Why, yes, I did," came the reply. "I said, 'Good afternoon.' How are you?"

"I'm fine, thank you," answered Dorothy politely. "How are you?"

"I'm not feeling well," said the Scarecrow with a groan, "for it is very tedious being perched up here night and day to scare away crows."

"Can't you get down?" asked Dorothy.

"No, for this pole is stuck up my back. If you will please take away the pole, I shall be greatly obliged to you."

Dorothy walked over to the Scarecrow and reached both arms up to lift him off the pole. Being stuffed with straw, he was quite light. As soon as he was on the ground, he gave a big stretch and

thanked Dorothy many times. “Who are you,” he asked, curiously “and where are you going?”

“My name is Dorothy. I’m going to the Emerald City to ask the wonderful Wizard of Oz to send me back to Kansas. Do you know where that is?”

“No, indeed,” said the Scarecrow sadly. “I don’t know anything. You see, I am stuffed, so I have no brains at all. If I went with you, do you think that Oz would give me some?”

“Well, it certainly can’t hurt to ask,” said Dorothy. “If he doesn’t, you wouldn’t be any worse off than you are now.”

Delighted by the idea, the Scarecrow decided to give it a try. So, once again, Dorothy set off down the road of yellow bricks, with Toto in her arms and her new friend, the Scarecrow, by her side.

Chapter 4

Into the Forest

Dorothy enjoyed walking with the Scarecrow. Having no brains, he often stepped into holes and fell flat on the hard bricks. It never hurt him, though, as he was made of straw. Dorothy would pick him up and set him upon his feet again, while he joined her, laughing merrily at his own mishap.

The farms here were not nearly so well cared for as they had been farther back. There were fewer houses and fewer fruit trees. The farther they went, the more dismal and lonesome the country became. Eventually, the trio came to a dark, dense forest. The trees were so big and close together that their branches met over the road of yellow bricks. It was almost completely dark underneath the trees, for the branches shut out the daylight, but Dorothy and her companion continued on bravely.

"Well," the Scarecrow said, "if the road goes in, it must come out."

"Anyone would know that," Dorothy remarked.

"Certainly; that is why *I* know it," said the Scarecrow. "If it required brains to figure out, I would never have said it."

The farther into the forest they went, the darker it got. After an hour or so, the light faded away completely, and they found themselves stumbling along in the darkness. Dorothy could not see at all, but Toto could, for some dogs see very well in the dark. The Scarecrow declared that he could see as well as by day, so Dorothy let them lead the way.

"If you see a house or any place where we can spend the night," she said, "you must tell me, for I'm tired and it is very uncomfortable walking in the dark."

Soon afterward, the Scarecrow stopped. "I see a little cottage built out of logs and branches over there, to the right of us," he said. "Shall we go there?"

"Yes, indeed," answered Dorothy, yawning. "I'm tired."

So the Scarecrow led her through the tall trees until they reached the cottage.

Dorothy entered and found a bed of dried leaves in one corner. She lay down at once and, with Toto beside her, soon fell into a sound sleep. The Scarecrow, who was never tired, stood in another corner, waiting patiently until morning came.

When Dorothy woke, the trio set off to look for water. They found a little spring, where Dorothy drank and washed her face and hands. As they headed back to the road, Dorothy heard a strange sound, like a squeaky groan. She searched until she found the source of the sound—a woodcutter made entirely of tin! He stood without moving an inch, his axe raised above his head. He looked as if he were rusted in place.

"Did you groan?" asked Dorothy.

"Yes, I did," replied the Tin Woodman, sadly. "I've been standing here for over a year and no one has helped me. I am mighty tired of standing here."

"What can we do to help?" she asked.

"Go get my oil can from my cottage

over there. If you oil my joints, then I'll be free to move again."

Dorothy raced through the trees to get the Tin Woodman's oil can. Minutes later, she was back in the clearing, and the Scarecrow helped her oil all of the Tin Woodman's joints. Finally, he could move again. He skipped around the clearing joyously celebrating his release. "Oh, thank you," the Tin Woodman cried. "I might have stood there forever if you hadn't helped me. What are you doing way out here, anyway?"

"We are traveling to the Emerald City to see the great Oz," Dorothy told him. "I'm going to ask him to send Toto and me back to Kansas, and the Scarecrow wants to ask him for a brain."

"Really?" asked the Tin Woodman. "Do you think that Oz could give me a heart? I am merely a hollow shell of a man with no heart."

"I don't see why not," said Dorothy. "It shouldn't be any harder than giving the Scarecrow a brain."

"Come along," said the Scarecrow, "we'll all go together."

"Yes," chimed in Dorothy. "It would be great to have your company."

So off the four of them went on their way, along the road of yellow bricks toward the Emerald City.

Chapter 5

The King of the Beasts

The woods continued to get darker and thicker. Walking was becoming more and more difficult. The companions had to watch the road carefully, and the Tin Woodman's axe came in handy as he helped clear the way. No birds chirped and no insects buzzed. The only sounds were the wind moaning in the trees and an occasional deep, scary growl from the forest. The friends walked as quickly as they could.

"How far is it to the edge of the forest?" asked Dorothy, glancing around fearfully.

"I'm not sure," said the Tin Woodman. "I never went there, but my father, who was also a woodcutter, told me that it's a very long journey through some bad areas. But I'm not afraid—as long as I have my oil can, nothing can hurt me. The Scarecrow is made of straw, so nothing can hurt him, either—"

"Except fire!" exclaimed the Scarecrow. "I'd go up in flames just like *that.*" He snapped his fingers cheerfully.

"And you, Dorothy," the Tin Woodman continued, "have been kissed by the Good Witch of the North, so nothing can hurt you, either."

"What about Toto?" Dorothy wanted to know. "What will protect him?"

"We will," the Tin Woodman replied.

At that moment, a deafening roar came from the trees and a huge creature burst out of the forest. With one swipe of its mighty paw, it flung the Scarecrow to the

ground. Straw flew everywhere, but the Tin Woodman bravely jumped into the fray. He, too, was knocked down with one swipe of the beast's paw, and he lay very still on the road. Then the beast turned to stare at Dorothy and Toto.

It was the biggest lion that Dorothy had ever seen. It was as big as a horse! Suddenly Toto, barking furiously, ran right at the lion. As the lion opened his huge mouth to gobble the little dog up, Dorothy dashed past Toto and slapped the lion on his nose as hard as she could.

"Don't you dare bite Toto!" Dorothy yelled at him. "A big beast like you should be ashamed of yourself for biting a poor, little dog."

"I didn't bite him," the lion wailed as he sat rubbing his nose.

"No, but you tried to," she snapped, going over to help the Scarecrow and Tin Woodman regain their senses. "You're just a big coward. Why don't you attack something your own size?"

"I know I'm a coward," cried the lion, sniffling and wiping his nose with his tail. "I'm sorry if I scared you."

"Why are you a coward?" Dorothy asked him.

"I don't know," he said. "I've *always* been a coward. I just roar and usually everyone runs away because they think that the King of the Beasts is brave."

"Well," said the Scarecrow, "we're going to the Emerald City and I'm going to ask the great Oz for a brain. The Tin Woodman wants a heart, and Dorothy and Toto want to go home to Kansas. Perhaps Oz could give you some courage."

"Do you really think so?" asked the Cowardly Lion hopefully.

"As easily as he could give me a brain," said the Scarecrow.

"Or me a heart," said the Tin Woodman.

"Or send Toto and me home to Kansas," said Dorothy.

"Then I think I'll go with you," said the lion, "if it's okay with you, of course. It's not any fun to be a coward all the time."

So the Cowardly Lion joined the group, which once again set off along the road of yellow bricks. They walked until it was dark, then stopped for the night under a huge tree in the forest. Dorothy and Toto slept snuggled under a blanket of soft, dry leaves.

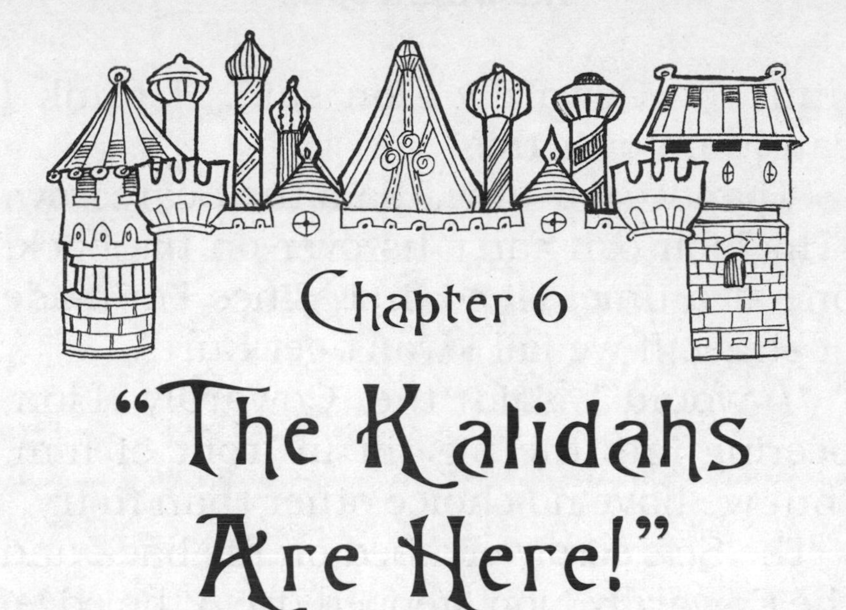

Chapter 6

"The Kalidahs Are Here!"

When the next morning came, it was still very dark under the trees. They began walking again, and soon came to a huge ditch that split the road. The ditch stretched as far as they could see to either side and it was very deep, with sharp rocks at the bottom. The sides were too steep to climb down or up.

"How are we going to cross it?" asked Dorothy in despair.

They all stood there and thought hard

until the Cowardly Lion said, "I think I can jump over this!"

"Then we'll be fine," said the Scarecrow. "The Lion can carry us over on his back, one at a time. I'll go first, since I'm made of straw. If we fall I won't get hurt."

"*I* would," said the Cowardly Lion, peering into the big rift in front of him, "but we have no choice other than to try."

The Scarecrow climbed on his back and the Cowardly Lion stepped up to the edge. The friends could see his muscles bunch up as he crouched. Then he leaped up and over as far as he could. He landed safely on the other side, and his friends all clapped and cheered.

"You did it!" shouted Dorothy. "That was very brave of you!"

The Lion jumped back across to get another passenger. "It's my turn now," said Dorothy as she scooped up Toto and climbed onto the Lion's back. After Dorothy and Toto, the Cowardly Lion carried the Tin Woodman over, and the group was together again.

They walkcd vcry cautiously now, because the woods were even gloomier on this side of the ditch. Strange noises came from all around them, and they huddled together as they walked.

"Oh, no. Oh, no," the Cowardly Lion whispered to his friends. "The Kalidahs live over here."

"What are Kalidahs?" asked Dorothy.

"They are nasty, horrible creatures

with bodies like bears and heads like tigers," the Cowardly Lion explained with a shudder. "They are vicious and could eat me as easily as I could eat Toto."

Just then, they arrived at another deep gap in the road. This one was so wide, the Lion couldn't jump over it. So, again, they all sat down to think about what to do. The Scarecrow soon spoke up.

"I know," he said. "The Tin Woodman can cut down this tree here so it falls across the gap. Then we can use it as a bridge and walk over on it." He finished by patting the trunk of a huge tree, which stood nearby.

"That's a great idea!" said the Cowardly Lion. "It almost makes me think that you have brains in your head instead of straw."

The Tin Woodman went to work and soon had the tree down and across the gap. They had just started to cross their makeshift bridge when a sharp growl came out of the forest behind them.

"What was that?" asked Dorothy.

"Th-th-the K-K-Kalidahs are here!" cried

the Cowardly Lion, beginning to shake and stammer. Indeed, two horrible beasts with bodies like bears and heads like tigers came bounding toward them.

"Run, before they catch us!" cried the Scarecrow.

Dorothy ran over first, with Toto in her arms. The Tin Woodman followed, with thc Scarecrow right on his heels. The Cowardly Lion, though, turned to face the Kalidahs and gave such a terrible roar that it scared even his companions. The Scarecrow was so surprised that he fell over. The Cowardly Lion took advantage of the Kalidahs' surprise and ran to join his friends. Unfortunately, the roar didn't stop the Kalidahs for long. Soon, they ran forward again, headed for the makeshift bridge.

"Stand behind me. Even though we are certainly done for, I will fight them as long as I can," declared the Cowardly Lion.

"Wait!" cried the Scarecrow. "Tin Woodman, use your axe to chop off the end of the tree on our side! Quickly!"

The Tin Woodman did so, as fast as he

could. By the time the tree was almost chopped through, the Kalidahs were only inches away. Just as the beasts were reaching for the friends, the Cowardly Lion pushed on the tree with all his weight. The tree snapped and fell into the chasm, taking the two snarling Kalidahs with it.

"Well," said the Cowardly Lion after a moment's silence, "I am glad that we arc going to live a while longer. I don't know if I've ever been so scared!"

Everyone agreed. They started down the road of yellow bricks again, even faster than before because they wanted to be out of the kalidahs' territory before night fell.

At long last, the trees got farther apart and sunlight filtered down through the branches again. They reached the end of the forest at dusk and camped for the night beside a wide, fast-running river.

Chapter 7

The Poppy Field

The next morning, the Tin Woodman made a raft for crossing the river. They boarded their craft and used poles to push it across the river. Everything was fine—until they got to the fast-moving center.

"The water is too deep!" exclaimed the surprised Scarecrow when his pole could no longer reach the bottom.

A swift current was sweeping their raft downstream, and the road of yellow bricks was getting farther and farther away. If they didn't get to the other side soon, the river would carry them into the lands ruled by the Wicked Witch of the West. She would make them all her slaves.

Desperate, the Cowardly Lion jumped into the water, telling Dorothy to grab his tail. He swam as hard as he could toward the bank. He struggled for several minutes before he got free of the current and could pull the little raft into shallow

water. They all breathed a sigh of relief, and the Lion climbed back on board to rest while the Tin Woodman and the Scarecrow pushed them the rest of the way to dry land.

Once ashore, they began to trek back upstream to find the road of yellow bricks. The land was beautiful on this side of the river and Dorothy ate juicy, delicious fruit from the trees along the way. They walked along listening to the singing of brightly colored birds, and enjoying the lovely flowers that were everywhere. Big clusters of flowers—bright yellow and white and blue and purple—dazzled Dorothy's eyes. Presently, they came upon a large field of red poppies.

"They're so beautiful," sighed Dorothy.

Her friends were worried, though, because they knew the secret of the poppies. The flowers had a perfume so strong, it made anyone who breathed it fall into a deep sleep that would last forever unless the sleeper was carried a safe distance away. But they had no choice—they had to cross the field. They made Dorothy run, but the field was too big. She fell down, asleep, with Toto in her arms.

"Oh, no," cried the Tin Woodman, wringing his hands. "What shall we do?"

"I'm getting so sleepy myself," mumbled the Cowardly Lion with a big yawn.

The Scarecrow and the Tin Woodman, who were not affected by the smell of the flowers, looked at each other in dismay.

"You'd better run ahead," the Scarecrow told the Cowardly Lion. "We can carry Dorothy and Toto, but you are too big for us. You must get out on your own." So the Cowardly Lion ran off as fast as he could.

Meanwhile, the Scarecrow and the Tin Woodman made a chair with their arms. They picked up Dorothy and Toto and slowly carried them out of the field. Near the field's edge, they found the Cowardly Lion fast asleep. He was only a few feet from safety. His two friends were very sad to see him there.

"We can do nothing for him," said the Tin Woodman. "He is much too heavy for us to lift. We'll have to leave him here to sleep forever. I hope that he will dream that he found his courage."

The Scarecrow had to agree. The two of them carried the slumbering Dorothy and Toto well away from the field and their dear friend, the Cowardly Lion.

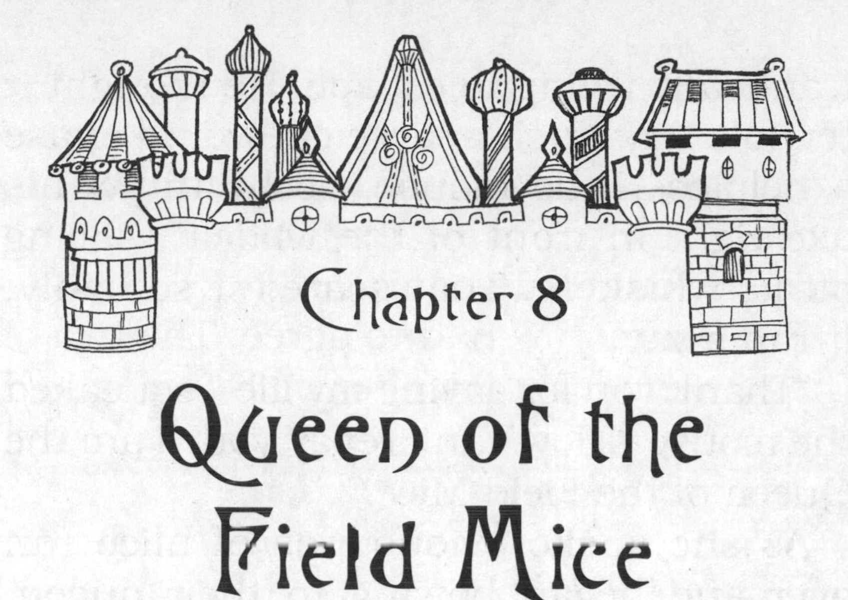

Chapter 8

Queen of the Field Mice

While the Tin Woodman and the Scarecrow were waiting patiently for Dorothy and Toto to wake up, they heard a low growl. The Tin Woodman, who could turn his head in a complete circle because of his hinges, looked behind them.

A ferocious-looking wildcat was running across the grass, right at them! The Tin Woodman thought the wildcat was after them until he saw a pretty, little field mouse just in front of the wildcat, frantically trying to escape. He thought it terrible that such a large cat would chase a helpless little mouse, so he threw his axe right in front of the wildcat, slicing off its whiskers. That scared it so badly, it ran away.

"Thank you for saving my life," squeaked the mouse. "How can I repay you? I am the Queen of the Field Mice."

As she spoke, thousands of mice ran over and began bowing to their queen. Toto, now awake, got so excited that he started barking and chasing mice just like he used to do in Kansas. The mice scattered instantly, so the Tin Woodman picked Toto up and held him tightly in

his arms. He told the Queen not to worry; she would be safe.

Timidly, the Queen of the Field Mice crept back, repeating her offer to help.

"I don't know of anything you could—" the Tin Woodman began, but the Scarecrow excitedly interrupted.

"Yes, there is!" he crowed. "Could you please help us get our friend the Cowardly Lion out of the poppy field? He is quite a scared fellow, so he won't hurt you. Besides, he's asleep from the scent of the poppies."

The Queen agreed, and everyone followed the Scarecrow's plan. The Tin Woodman built a platform big enough for the Cowardly Lion, and made wheels for it. The mice ran off to get one piece of string each. Then they tied themselves to the new cart and pulled it to the field of poppies. When they got to the Cowardly Lion, the Scarecrow and the Tin Woodman pushed and pulled on him until they finally managed to get him onto the cart.

Right away, the mice began to pull, but nothing happened. They pulled with all their might, but the Cowardly Lion was just too heavy. They were in trouble, because now the mice were beginning to tire from the smell of the poppies. One last time, the Tin Woodman and the Scarecrow pushed while the mice pulled yet again. The cart moved a little, then a little more. Then it started to roll faster and faster. They reached the edge of the field and kept going until they reached Dorothy, who was finally awake. She was amazed at the sight coming toward her.

The Queen of the Field Mice was still grateful to the Tin Woodman for saving her life, so she gave him a tiny whistle to call her with if he ever needed her again. Then the mice left, and the Cowardly Lion's friends waited for him to wake up.

Chapter 9
The Guardian of the Gates

With a great stretch and a yawn, the Cowardly Lion finally woke up. He had slept quite a while because he had lain in the poppies for so long. Neither he nor Dorothy thought that the poppies were quite so beautiful anymore.

They started walking again and soon found the road of yellow bricks. They were overjoyed to see it. The road was nicely paved and cared for once again—just as it had been in the land of the Munchkins.

All day they followed the road. While they walked, they passed neat little farms. The people wore clothing like that of the Munchkins, but here everything was green rather than blue. The green people sometimes came out to look, but they wouldn't talk because they were afraid of the Cowardly Lion. The four friends walked quickly, stopping to rest for only a few minutes at a time.

The day wore on into the afternoon. Finally, on the horizon, they saw a green glow in the sky. Soon afterward, they could see the walls of the Emerald City. What a breathtaking sight! The friends walked much faster and soon reached the walls. Huge gates, studded with brilliant emeralds, stood at the end of the road of yellow bricks. There, they stopped and rang a bell.

The gates creaked open ever so slowly. Beyond them stood a little man dressed entirely in green. Even his skin had a greenish tint to it.

"Why do you wish to enter the Emerald City?" he asked them.

"We've come to see the Great Oz," answered Dorothy.

The man was so surprised by her answer that he sat down, shaking his head. "It has been a long time since anyone came to see Oz," he said. "If he believes that you have come for a silly reason, he may destroy you on the spot."

"But we *haven't* come for a silly reason," declared the Scarecrow, "and we were told that Oz is a very good wizard."

"Oh, he is," the green man reassured them. "He rules the Emerald City wisely, but he does not treat people with foolish requests nicely. Few are brave enough to ask to see him. As the Guardian of the Gates, I will take you to the palace. However, you must wear special glasses while you are in the Emerald City."

"Why?" asked Dorothy.

"Because the beauty and brightness of our city will blind you if you don't wear

them. Even those of us who live here wear them." He pulled out a box full of keys and eyeglasses with green shades in various sizes and shapes. He locked a pair onto everyone's head—even Toto's—and put the keys back in the box. Then the Guardian of the Gates took a different key, a big, golden one from his pocket, and unlocked another gate. He went through it first, and the companions followed him into the Emerald City.

Chapter 10

The Emerald City of Oz

The Emerald City was astonishing. Everything was green—even the rays of sunlight pouring into the city. Emeralds sparkled from the walls, from the streets and sidewalks, and from every shop window along the way. It was dazzling, and the friends were glad that they wore protective eyeglasses. The people of the city watched them, but kept their distance because of the Cowardly Lion.

At last, they reached the palace of Oz,

which was in the exact center of the city. There, the Guardian of the Gates stopped to talk with a soldier with green whiskers, who was standing at the door.

"I bring strangers who wish to see the Great Oz," the Guardian of the Gates told the soldier.

The soldier looked surprised, but spoke politely, saying, "Please step inside. I will go tell Oz of your request. Make yourselves comfortable." He pointed to several

comfortable-looking couches set along the wall. They all sat on the couches, except for the Cowardly Lion and Toto, who were more comfortable on the floor, and waited. They sat for a long time, getting more nervous by the minute. What was taking so long? What if Oz refused to see them?

By the time the soldier returned, Dorothy was so nervous that she jumped up and blurted out, "Did you see Oz?"

"Oh, no," answered the soldier, "I have never seen him. But I did tell him that you want to see him, and he agreed to let you do so—one at a time. He will see you first," he pointed at Dorothy, "tomorrow morning. He will see only one of you a day, so we will find a comfortable room for each of you to sleep in."

This wasn't exactly the news that they were hoping for, but at least they hadn't been turned away. A beautiful girl with green hair and skin arrived to lead them to their rooms, one at a time. Dorothy went first and, after rummaging around in a closet full of gorgeous green dresses, she fell asleep on the plush, green bed with Toto by her side.

In the morning, the green girl returned. She had Dorothy put on a dress from the closet, then follow her down to breakfast. There, Dorothy rejoined her friends, but not for long. The soldier came in and told her it was time to go meet Oz. He led her to the door of Oz's throne room, told her that she must go in by herself, and left.

Hesitantly, she stepped through the door and closed it behind her. When she turned around slowly to look at the throne room because she had never been in one before, she almost cried out. There, above a gigantic throne, hovered an enormous, hairless head, with no body, arms, or legs. It was bigger than the head of the biggest giant.

"I am Oz, the Great and Terrible," the head declared. "Who are you and why do you wish to see me?"

Dorothy took a deep breath. The voice,

she decided, was not as awful as she had expected from the big head. So she curtsied and answered, “I am Dorothy, the small and meek. I have come to ask you to help my dog and me get back home to Kansas. Your land seems very nice, but it isn’t my home and I am sure that Aunt Em and Uncle Henry must be terribly worried about me by now.”

“Why should I do that for you?” demanded the head.

“Because you are strong and I am weak, and you are a great wizard, while I am only a young girl.”

The head considered her response. Its eyes blinked up at the ceiling, down to the floor, then around in its head. It did this for several minutes. Then the eyes looked back at Dorothy again.

“Where did you get those silver shoes?” the head questioned suddenly.

“I got them from the Wicked Witch of the East. My house fell on her and killed her,” Dorothy replied.

"Where did you get that mark upon your forehead?"

"From the Good Witch of the North when she kissed me at the beginning of my journey. She sent me to you."

The giant head rolled its huge eyes around again, then declared, "I will give you my answer now. In my country, we do not do favors for each other. Everyone must pay for what he or she gets. Therefore, I will not send you to Kansas until you have done something for me."

"What must I do?" asked the girl.

"You must kill the Wicked Witch of the West," thundered Oz.

"I can't do that!" exclaimed a dismayed Dorothy. "I don't want to hurt anyone."

"You killed the Wicked Witch of the East—"

"By accident," Dorothy interrupted. "My house fell on her."

"—and you wear the silver shoes, which have a powerful charm," Oz continued, "and you have the Good Witch's mark on your forehead. There is only one wicked witch left, and I want her gone."

"If you're so powerful, why can't *you* do it?" questioned Dorothy.

"I may be able to," replied Oz, "but that is what you must do for me if you want me to do something for you. Leave me now and do not return until you can prove that the witch is dead."

Dorothy left the throne room in tears. When she returned to her friends, she told them what the wizard had said. Then she went to her room to be by herself. She didn't believe that she would ever see her home again.

Chapter 11

The Many Faces of Oz

The next morning, the Scarecrow bravely entered the throne room. He was expecting to find the huge head. Instead, he saw a beautiful fairy. Her wings and hair were bright green, and she had a crown of perfect emeralds on her head.

"I am Oz, the Great and Terrible," she said. "Who are you and why do you wish to see me?"

"I am a Scarecrow, with a head full of

straw," came the reply. "I ask you to give me brains so I will be like other men."

"Why should I do that for you?" Oz demanded.

"Because you are wise and powerful, and no one else can help," was the reply.

"Well, I do not grant favors. If you kill the Wicked Witch of the West, I will give you enough brains to make you the wisest man in all of Oz. Now go and do not return until the witch is dead."

The Scarecrow hurried from the throne room and went to tell his friends about his meeting. He was quite sad that he hadn't received any brains.

The next morning, it was the Tin Woodman's turn. He hoped to find the beautiful fairy, since he thought that she would be more likely than the head to give him a heart. Once inside the room, however, he stopped and stared. Upon the throne was a huge, shaggy beast. It had five arms, five legs, and five eyes in a head something like a rhinoceros's. It was a terrible-looking beast but, being made of tin, the Tin Woodman was not afraid of it.

"I am Oz, the Great and Terrible," roared the beast. "Who are you and why do you wish to see me?"

"I am a woodman made of tin, but with no heart," was the reply. "I cannot love, so I have come to ask you for a heart."

"Why should I do that for you?" Oz demanded.

"Because I ask it, and because you

alone are powerful enough to grant my request," the Tin Woodman said bravely.

"If you want a heart," growled the beast, "you must earn it. Help Dorothy and the Scarecrow kill the Wicked Witch of the West. Bring me proof, and you shall receive the kindest heart in Oz."

The Tin Woodman left and told his friends what Oz had said.

The Cowardly Lion was the only one who had not yet seen Oz. He decided that if he met the head, he would roll it around the room until he was granted his wish. If he met the fairy, he would jump at her and scare her until she gave it to him. If he met the beast, he would roar until he rattled it so much that it gave him his courage. He fell asleep dreaming of the courage he would gain the next day.

The next morning, he rushed into the throne room, ready for any of the three faces of Oz. Again, however, Oz was in a new form—an immense flame so hot and bright that the Cowardly Lion had to shield his face and creep back against the

far wall. This was not at all what he had expected, so he began to shake with fear.

A quiet voice came from the ball. “I am Oz, the Great and Terrible,” it said. “Who are you and why do you wish to see me?”

“I am a Cowardly Lion,” came the reply, “and I ask that you grant me courage so that I can truly be the King of the Beasts.”

Oz thought a moment, then said, “Help the others kill the Wicked Witch of the West and bring me proof. If you do not, you will remain a coward forever.”

The Cowardly Lion was angry at the answer, but had no reply. He glared at the ball of fire, but it kept getting hotter, until he could bear it no longer. He ran from the throne room to tell his friends the news.

They were worried and upset, but decided that they must not quit. They had to at least *try* to kill the Wicked Witch of the West, so they began to prepare for their next journey.

Chapter 12

The New Journey

When morning came, a soldier led the friends to the gates of the city. There, the Guardian of the Gates unlocked and put away their glasses. Then he opened the outer gate.

"How do we find the Wicked Witch of the West?" Dorothy asked him.

"There is no road, because no one ever wants to go there," he said.

"We do," said the Scarecrow. "We're going there to destroy her."

"Oh," said the Guardian. "That's different. Keep walking west, where the sun sets, and she will find *you*. She makes everyone in the west her slave."

Soon, the city was far behind them and the ground was rocky and hilly. There were no houses or farms, and it was extremely hot. There were no trees for shade, and the ground was hard. The sun beat down on them all morning. It made Dorothy, Toto, and the Cowardly Lion so tired that they had to lie down and rest. The Tin Woodman and the Scarecrow watched over them.

Meanwhile, far to the west, the Wicked Witch was sitting outside her castle, surveying her kingdom. She had only one eye, but it was as powerful as a telescope. She could see everything in her kingdom. When she looked around, she spotted Dorothy and her friends. The Wicked Witch was very angry that they had dared to enter her kingdom. She blew hard on a silver whistle she wore around her neck, summoning a snarling pack of big, gray

wolves. They had long legs, fierce eyes, and extremely sharp teeth.

"Go find those strangers and tear them apart!" commanded the Wicked Witch.

"Aren't you going to make them slaves, the way you usually do?" asked the wolf pack's leader.

"No," snapped the Wicked Witch. "They would not make very good slaves. One is made of tin, one is made of straw, and the lion is a coward. That leaves a weak girl and her silly little dog."

At that, the leader dashed off with his pack just behind him, howling like mad.

They ran as fast as the wind and reached the companions in just a few moments.

Luckily, the Scarecrow and the Tin Woodman saw them coming.

"Let me handle this," said the Tin Woodman, stepping in front of the Scarecrow and their sleeping friends.

When the wolves reached the Tin Woodman, he swung his axe and chopped off the first wolf's head. The rest of the pack came at him from every side, snarling and biting and clawing, but he was made of tin, so he wasn't hurt. Soon, the entire pack was dead, and the Tin Woodman's weary companions had not even woken up.

Chapter 13

The Wicked Witch Strikes Again

When Dorothy and the Cowardly Lion woke up the next morning, they were surprised to see all the dead wolves. The Tin Woodman told his friends what had happened, and they thanked him for saving their lives. After a bite of breakfast, the little group headed west again.

Just then, the Wicked Witch of the West used her magic eye to see what had become of her wolves. When she saw that they were all dead and the friends were still trespassing in her kingdom, she flew into a rage. She blew twice on her silver whistle, and immediately, a flock of wild crows surrounded her.

"Fly at once to those strangers," she shrieked. "Peck out their eyes and rip them to pieces!"

Off the crows flew toward the friends. They were frightened by the sight of the huge cawing flock, which was big enough to darken the sky.

"Let me take care of this," said the Scarecrow. He told his friends to lie on the ground around him and cover their heads with their arms. The Scarecrow stood above them and put his arms out to either side, as if he were stuck on a pole.

Crows are always afraid of scarecrows, and these birds were no different. When they saw him they changed their course. They flew in circles around him, but they were too afraid to fly any closer.

The King Crow, who was bigger and smarter than the others, looked more

closely and saw that the Scarecrow was only stuffed with straw. He called to his followers, "It is only a stuffed man. Peck his eyes out!"

The King Crow flew at the Scarecrow's face, but the Scarecrow fought back by snatching the king out of the air and twisting his neck. The other crows flew at the Scarecrow in a fury, trying to rip out his stuffing, but he was too quick for them. He caught each one and twisted its neck. Soon, the whole flock of crows lay dead on the ground.

The grateful friends got up and thanked the Scarecrow for saving their lives. Then they started walking west yet again.

Back at the castle, the Wicked Witch had watched the whole scene. She was even angrier now than when she had discovered that her wolves were dead. This time, she blew on her silver whistle three times. A loud buzz filled the air and, seconds later, a swarm of big black bees hovered around her.

"Go find the strangers and sting them to death!" the Wicked Witch ordered. The swarm buzzed away at once.

The Tin Woodman saw the bees coming and warned his friends. Again, the Scarecrow knew just what to do.

"Lie down quickly," he told Dorothy, Toto, and the Cowardly Lion. "Now," he told the Tin Woodman, "take out my stuffing and spread it over them as thickly as you can. The bees won't be able to sting them through the straw."

They obeyed the Scarecrow and finished just as the bees arrived. The only stranger the bees could see was the Tin Woodman. When they tried to sting him, they couldn't hurt him because he was made of tin. All that happened was that the bees' stingers broke off. Of course, bees can't live after they sting someone, so pretty soon all the bees were dead.

Dorothy and the Cowardly Lion got up and filled the Scarecrow with his stuffing. They thanked the Scarecrow and Tin Woodman for once again saving their lives.

When the Wicked Witch saw what had happened to her bees, she was angrier than ever before. Three of her most powerful weapons were defeated because of a tin woodman with no heart, a scarecrow with no brains, a lion with no courage, and a girl with a little dog. The Wicked Witch stamped her feet and threw things around until she thought of a new plan. She ordered forty of her slaves, the Winkies, to kill the strangers. She gave them all sharp spears and sent them off.

The Winkies had to do what the Wicked Witch said, but they weren't very brave. When they got close to the strangers, the Cowardly Lion jumped in front of his friends, let out a terrible roar, and raked the air with his claws. The Winkies were so frightened that they dropped their spears and ran away as fast as they could.

Now, the Wicked Witch was angrier than she had ever been in her entire life. The group of strangers was still in her kingdom, her first three plans had been thwarted, and forty of her slaves had run away in a panic. She had to find a way to stop the intruders. Then she remembered her Golden Cap.

Chapter 14

The Golden Cap

The Golden Cap, which was kept in a special cabinet, had magic powers. It was made of gleaming gold, with a circle of diamonds and rubies running around it. Whoever owned the cap could use it three times to call the Winged Monkeys, and the Winged Monkeys would do as the owner commanded.

The Wicked Witch had used the charm twice already. The first time, she ordered the Winged Monkeys to help her make the Winkies her slaves. The second time, she got the monkeys to fight Oz and chase him out of her kingdom. She didn't want to use her third command until she absolutely had to, but there didn't seem to be any other way to stop the intruders.

The Wicked Witch opened the cabinet, took out the cap, and put it on her head. She stood on her left foot, then she stood on her right foot, then she made her wish and bowed.

At once, the sky grew dark and a loud rumble seemed to come from everywhere. Soon she was surrounded by huge, Winged Monkeys.

The biggest Winged Monkey, who seemed to be their leader, flew close to the Wicked Witch and said, "This is the third and last time you can call us. What do you command?"

The Wicked Witch pointed toward Dorothy and her friends and said, "Go there and destroy them all, except the lion. Bring him to me, and I shall har-

ness him like a horse and put him to work as my slave."

"As you command," said the leader. The Winged Monkeys flew away in a big, dark cloud of chattering noise.

They flew so fast that the friends had no chance to prepare for the attack. In a flash, the Winged Monkeys had taken the axe from the Tin Woodman and carried him away. They carried him very high over a gully full of sharp rocks. Then they dropped him. He landed on the rocks with a crash and lay there, dented and broken and unable to move. As he watched the Winged Monkeys fly away, he cried because he hadn't been able to help his friends. He thought that he would never

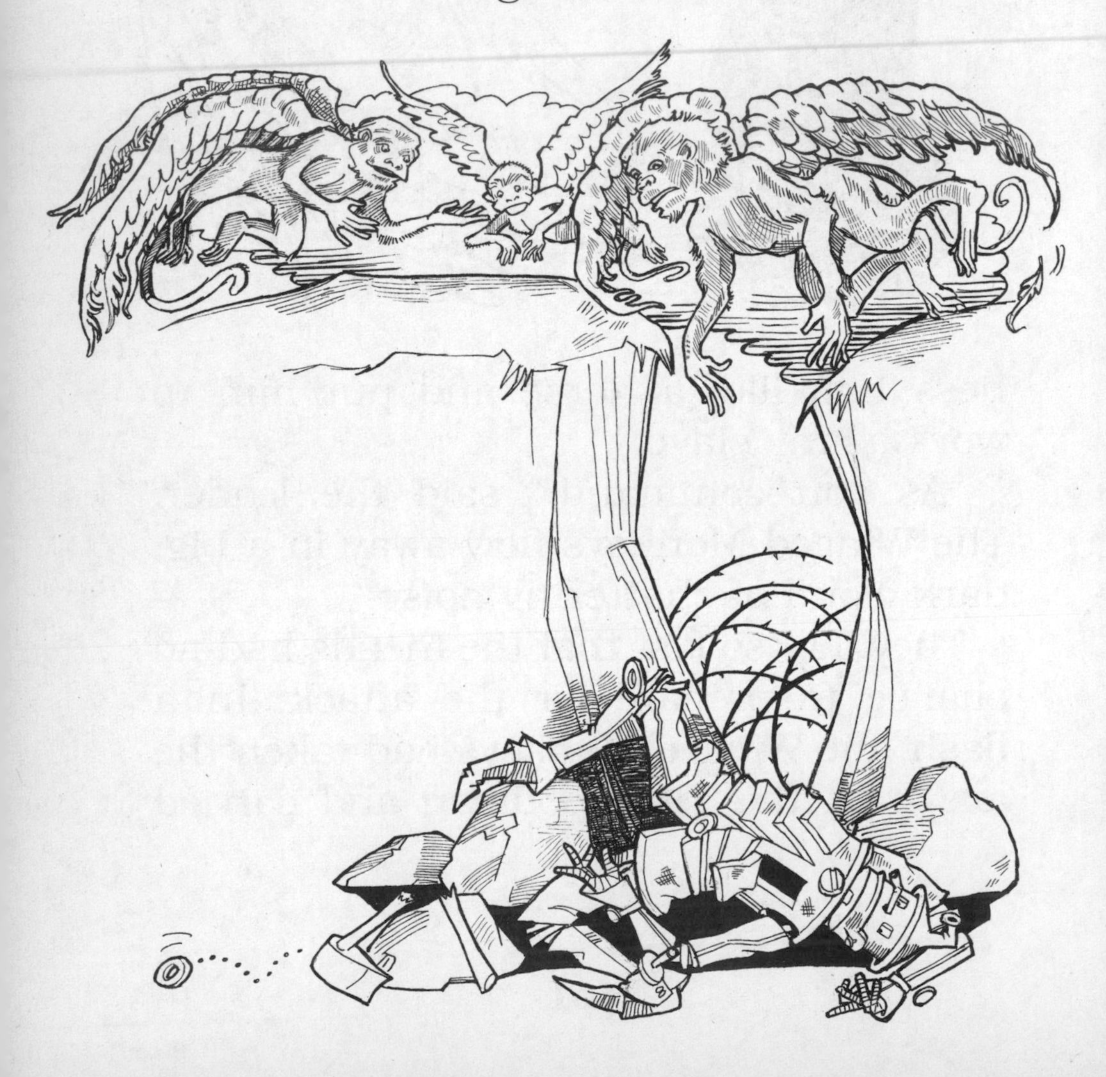

move again or get his heart. He couldn't dry his tears, so he slowly rusted. He couldn't even call for help.

Meanwhile, other Winged Monkeys were attacking the Scarecrow. They tore out all of his stuffing and threw it far out of reach. Then they took his clothes and threw them in the top of a tall tree. Without his stuffing, he was powerless to help his friends.

Still other monkeys were attacking the Lion. He growled and bit and jumped, but that wasn't enough to stop the Winged Monkeys. They threw ropes around his legs and neck until he couldn't move. Then they picked him up and flew away.

That left Dorothy and Toto all alone. The poor girl was upset about her friends and wondered what the Monkeys would do to her and Toto. But the Winged Monkeys did nothing at all. The leader had spotted the mark of the Good Witch's kiss on her forehead and told the others to stay back.

"This girl is protected by the Power of Good," he told his followers, "and that is greater than the power of evil. Let's just take her back to the Wicked Witch's castle and leave her there."

So that is what they did.

Back at the castle, the Winged Monkeys' leader told the Wicked Witch what had happened. "So that's it!" he said, dusting off his paws after setting Dorothy down. "You have no more power over us. Goodbye!" Then the Winged Monkeys took off. In just a few seconds, they were gone.

Chapter 15

The Witch's Castle

At first, the Wicked Witch of the West didn't know what to do with Dorothy. Once she saw the mark on Dorothy's forehead, she knew that she couldn't hurt the girl in any way. Then she looked at Dorothy's feet and saw the silver shoes. Oh, no! The Wicked Witch knew what a powerful charm was attached to them. Why hadn't the girl used their power already?

At first, this made the Wicked Witch

afraid of Dorothy. But once she looked in the girl's eyes, she felt better. The child had no idea how powerful the shoes were!

"She doesn't know how to use them!" the Wicked Witch thought to herself with glee. "If she did, I would already be gone! I can't take those shoes off her feet, but I will make her my slave. I'll soon find a way to trick her into giving me those shoes."

The Wicked Witch gave Dorothy a mean and scary look, and growled, "Come with me, girl, and do everything I tell you. If you don't, I'll make sure you end up just like the Scarecrow and the Tin Woodman!" The Wicked Witch took Dorothy to the kitchen and put her to work.

For weeks, the Wicked Witch made Dorothy scrub pots and sweep floors and keep the fireplace supplied with firewood. Dorothy always did what she was told. She was afraid of what the Wicked Witch might do to her if she didn't.

While Dorothy worked, the Wicked Witch would go see the Cowardly Lion.

She tried to harness him like a horse, but he wouldn't let her get close to him. She tried to starve him into obeying her, but that didn't work. The Wicked Witch didn't know that, every night, Dorothy sneaked out of the castle to visit her friend and take him something to eat. They would talk sadly of the Scarecrow and the Tin Woodman, and try to figure out a way to escape from this awful place.

Meanwhile, the Wicked Witch was trying to figure out how to get her hands on Dorothy's silver shoes. She waited, but Dorothy never took off the shoes except when she was in the bath. The Wicked Witch never went near Dorothy then, because she was deathly afraid of water.

Finally, the Wicked Witch came up with a plan. She put a bar of iron in the middle of the kitchen floor, then put a spell on it to make it invisible. It worked; while Dorothy was mopping the kitchen

floor the next day, she tripped over the invisible bar and fell so hard that one of her shoes went flying off her foot.

Cackling with joy, the Wicked Witch ran over and grabbed the shoe and stuck it on her own skinny foot.

Dorothy was so surprised at what had happened, and so upset at losing her shoe, she forgot to be afraid. "Give back my shoe!" she demanded.

"I will not!" crowed the Wicked Witch. "It's mine now, not yours, and someday soon I'll get the other one too." The Wicked Witch was very pleased to see that Dorothy still had no idea how to use the power of the remaining silver shoe on her foot. With one shoe in her possession, the Wicked Witch was sure that she would be able to use its special power to get the other one away from Dorothy.

"You are a wicked creature!" Dorothy cried. "Give me back that shoe. It's mine, not yours—the Good Witch of the North gave it to me!"

But the Wicked Witch just laughed and danced around Dorothy gleefully. This made Dorothy so furious that, without stopping to think, she picked up the bucket of water she was using and threw it on the Wicked Witch. In no time, the Wicked Witch went from cackling to screaming in fear. Then, to Dorothy's amazement, the Wicked Witch of the West began to melt.

"See what you've done!" the Wicked Witch screamed.

"I'm sorry!" wailed Dorothy, frightened by the sight. She had never meant to hurt anyone—not even a Wicked Witch.

"Didn't you know that water would be the end of me?" cried the Wicked Witch.

"Of course not," was Dorothy's reply. "How could I?"

"Oh," moaned the Wicked Witch, "in a moment I shall melt completely away and you will have my castle all to yourself. Oh, my! I certainly never thought that a weak girl like you would be the one to end my wicked deeds forever. Look out! Here I go!"

The Wicked Witch was gone, indeed. All that remained were a wet brown spot on the floor and Dorothy's silver shoe.

Dorothy cleaned off the shoe and put it back on her own foot. Then, with Toto close at her heels, she ran to tell the Cowardly Lion what had happened. The Wicked Witch of the West was dead, and they were free!

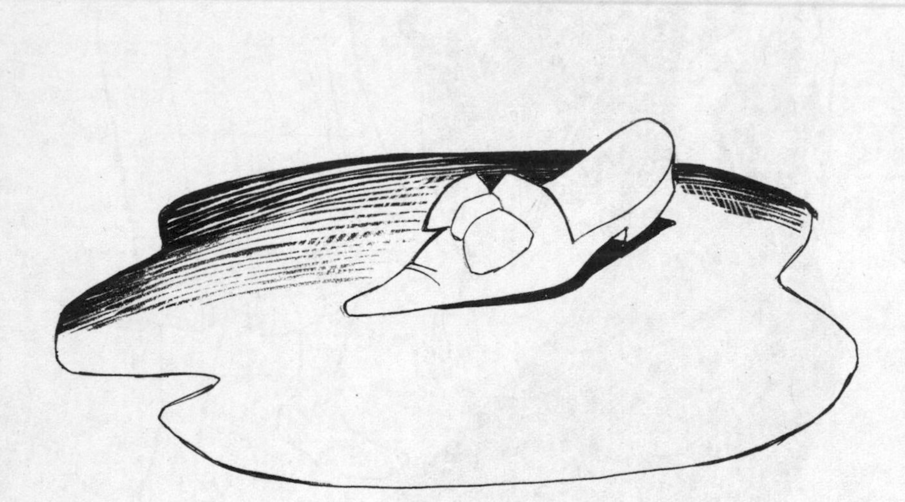

Chapter 16

Together Again

The Cowardly Lion was so happy to be free again. He followed Dorothy into the castle, where she called all of the Winkies together. Dorothy told them that she had accidentally melted the witch, so they were not her slaves any longer.

The Winkies were overjoyed. They had been slaves for such a long time, they could hardly believe that they were free. They threw a big party in Dorothy's honor that lasted for days. Dorothy and the Cowardly Lion enjoyed themselves at first. As the days went by, however, they kept thinking of the friends they had lost.

"If only the Scarecrow and the Tin Woodman could be here with us!" the Cowardly Lion exclaimed one afternoon. "If they were here, I could be very happy, courage or no courage."

"Do you think there is any chance that we could rescue them?" Dorothy asked.

"I don't know," the Cowardly Lion replied, "but it can't hurt to try."

So Dorothy asked the Winkies if they would be willing to help her.

"Of course!" the grateful Winkies cried. "We would do everything in our power to help the person who set us free! What would you like us to do?"

Dorothy told them what had happened to her friends and how much she wanted to find and rescue them.

In no time, Dorothy, the Cowardly Lion, and a large group of Winkies set out to search for the Tin Woodman. They searched all that day and part of the next.

At last, they came upon the rocky valley where the Tin Woodman lay, in a battered, bent, and rusty heap. Nearby was his trusty axe, with its blade rusted and its handle broken in half.

Very gently, the Winkies gathered up all the pieces of the Tin Woodman and his axe and carried them back to the Wicked Witch's castle.

"Are any of your people tinsmiths?" Dorothy asked the Winkies.

"Oh, yes," they said. The tinsmiths came at once, took a look at what was left of the Tin Woodman, and told Dorothy not to worry. "We'll soon have him as good as new!"

For four nights and three days, the Winkie tinsmiths worked hard. They welded the Tin Woodman's broken parts back together, banged out his dents, sanded and oiled away his rusty spots, and patched up the holes. Then, for the final touch, they polished him to a gleaming shine.

When the Tin Woodman could move and talk again, he thanked the Winkies. They took him to see Dorothy and the Cowardly Lion, who greeted him with shouts of joy. The Tin Woodman was so happy that he burst into tears. Dorothy wiped them away quickly, so he wouldn't rust again. The friends rejoiced at being together again, but they were saddened that the Scarecrow wasn't with them. "We have to try to find him," said Dorothy, and the others agreed.

The next day, Dorothy, Toto, the Cowardly Lion, the Tin Woodman, and a group of Winkies set out to find the Scarecrow. They walked all that day and part of the next day. At last, they came to a tall tree with straw scattered all around it. Looking up into the high branches, they saw the Scarecrow's clothes still where the Winged Monkeys had tossed them.

The tree was too tall and smooth for Dorothy or any of the Winkies to climb, but the Tin Woodman told them not to worry. "Stand back," he said. "I'll chop the tree down."

The Winkie tinsmiths had done as fine a job of fixing the Tin Woodman's axe as they had of fixing the Tin Woodman. The axe was so sharp that it took no time at all for the Tin Woodman to chop clean through the tree's thick trunk. The tree fell over with a crash, knocking the Scarecrow's clothes out of the branches they had been tangled in.

Very gently, the Winkies gathered up

every bit of the Scarecrow's body and clothes and carried them back to the Wicked Witch's castle. At once, the Winkies set about sewing up the ripped places and stuffing him with fresh, clean straw. In no time, he was as good as new. He hugged his friends and all the Winkies, thanking them over and over for saving him.

Now that they were all together again, the friends relaxed at the castle, celebrating with the Winkies and enjoying one another's company. After a few days, though, Dorothy began to feel homesick

again. More than anything, she wished that she could see her Aunt Em.

"We have to go back to the Emerald City," she said. "I want to ask Oz to keep his promise to send me back to Kansas."

"Yes," agreed the Tin Woodman. "The Wicked Witch of the West is dead, just as he commanded, and he promised to give me a heart in return."

"That's right," said the Scarecrow. "He promised to give me some brains."

"That's not all," said the Cowardly Lion. "He promised to give me courage."

They called the Winkies together again to tell them that they would be leaving the next morning. This made the Winkies very sad. They would miss all of their new friends, but they would especially miss the Tin Woodman, who had won their hearts. They begged him to stay and rule over their Yellow Land of the West.

"That would be a great honor," said the Tin Woodman, "but I really must go and ask Oz for a heart."

The Winkies understood. The next morning, they helped Dorothy gather supplies for the journey back to the Emerald City.

While searching for food to take with them, Dorothy opened a cabinet and discovered the Golden Cap and tried it on. It fit her perfectly! She didn't know anything about its magic powers, but she thought it was pretty.

"It belonged to the Wicked Witch," the Winkies told her. "Take it. It's yours!" So she put the Golden Cap on her head as she waved good-bye to the Winkies and set off with her friends on the journey back to Oz. As they walked away, the Winkies gave three loud cheers and shouted many good wishes for the companions to carry with them.

Chapter 17

Back to the Emerald City

The trip back to Oz was not going the way the friends had hoped. Although there was no road to follow, they knew that they had to keep walking east, toward where the sun rises. But for how long? Their journey from the Emerald City to the Wicked Witch's castle had been cut short by the Winged Monkeys, which had carried them swiftly through the air.

After Dorothy and her friends had walked for several days with no sign of the Emerald City, they began to grow very tired and discouraged. The sun had been hidden by clouds, so they weren't even sure they were going in the right direction.

One day, when they had stopped to rest, everyone was quiet. The Scarecrow, who was usually quite cheerful, began to grumble. "We have lost our way, I'm sure of it! If we keep wandering about like this, I shall never get my brains!"

"Nor I my heart!" said the Tin Woodman. "You must admit that this is taking a very long time, indeed!"

"So long," agreed the Cowardly Lion, "that I may never get any courage."

Everyone stared at Dorothy, even Toto, as if they expected her to do something. She was about to lose hope, when suddenly, she remembered someone who might help them.

"Tin Woodman!" she said, excitedly. "Where is the tiny whistle that the Queen of the Field Mice gave you? If we call her, perhaps she will be able to help us. She said that if we ever needed her, to blow the whistle and she would come!"

"Yes!" agreed the Scarecrow. "They are sure to know where the Emerald City is. I would have thought of that before if I had some brains!"

The Tin Woodman gave Dorothy the whistle, which she put in her mouth and blew. Just a few minutes later, they heard the pattering of tiny feet and hundreds of little gray mice came running up to them. The Queen herself came forward and said, in her squeaky, little voice, "What can I do for you, my friends?"

"Can you tell us how to get to the Emerald City?" asked Dorothy. "We have lost our way, and we desperately need to see Oz."

"Yes, I know where it is," the Queen replied, "but it is very far from here. You have been walking the wrong way." The Queen thought for a moment, then went on. "We are too small to help you get there quickly, but you can take care of that yourself. Why don't you use the Golden Cap to call the Winged Monkeys? They can carry you there in a few minutes."

"The Golden Cap?" said Dorothy in amazement. "I didn't know that it was a charm. But won't the Winged Monkeys hurt us again?"

"Oh, no!" the Queen of the Field Mice exclaimed. "They must obey whoever wears the cap. The charm is written inside the band. Just follow the instructions, and they will come and do whatever you wish. We must leave now though, because they like to chase us." Then she and her followers scurried off.

Dorothy took off the Golden Cap and looked inside. Sure enough, she saw a set of instructions. Dorothy did just as they said. First she stood on her left foot, then she stood on her right foot, then she made her wish and bowed.

Immediately the sky filled with a big, dark cloud. The Winged Monkeys had arrived! They crowded around Dorothy, happy that they wouldn't have to do evil things anymore. Their leader bowed low to Dorothy and said, "Hail, owner of the Golden Cap! We will grant you three wishes. What is your first command?"

"We wish to go to the Emerald City, but we have lost our way," Dorothy explained. "Can you take us there?"

"Of course," said the leader of the Winged Monkeys. "We can fly you there in less than an hour." Then, noticing how nervous the Tin Woodman, Scarecrow, and Cowardly Lion looked, he added, "Don't worry; we won't hurt you!"

Very gently, the Winged Monkeys picked up Dorothy and her friends and started flying toward the Emerald City. The Scarecrow and the Tin Woodman were

still nervous at first, but the Winged Monkeys were friendly and told them stories, so they soon relaxed and enjoyed the ride. In no time at all, they reached the gates of the Emerald City, where the Winged Monkeys set everyone down, said good-bye, then noisily flew away.

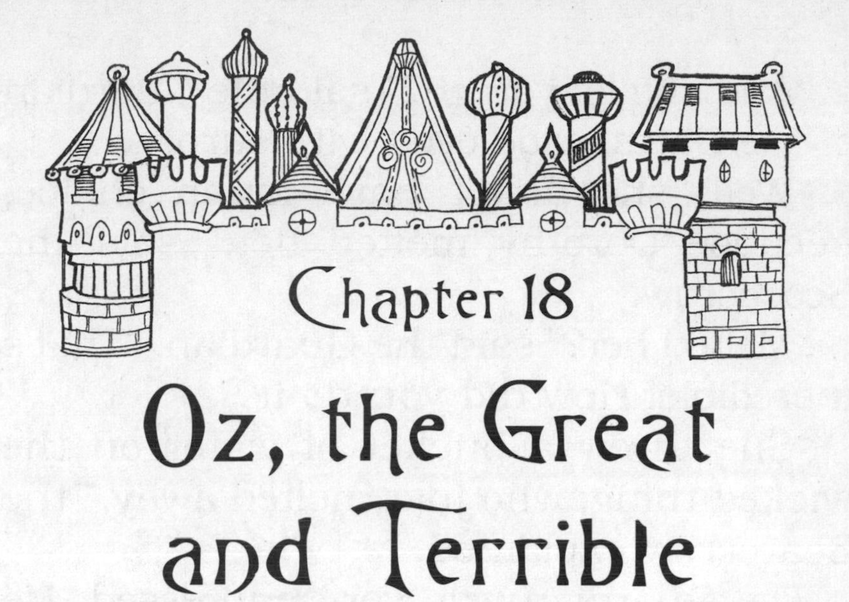

Chapter 18

Oz, the Great and Terrible

Dorothy rang the bell at the gates of the city, just as before. A few minutes later, just as before, the gates creaked open ever so slowly. Beyond them stood the Guardian of the Gates. He stared at them in surprise.

"You're back!" he exclaimed. "I thought that you went to the castle of the Wicked Witch of the West."

"We did," said the Scarecrow, as cheerfully as if it had been a stroll in the park.

"And she let you go?" said the Guardian of the Gates, wide-eyed with surprise.

"Well, she didn't have much choice, because Dorothy melted her," said the Scarecrow.

"Melted her?" said the Guardian. "That's incredible! How did you do it?"

"She threw a bucket of water on the wicked thing, who just melted away," the Scarecrow explained.

The Guardian was very impressed. He bowed very low to Dorothy. Then he invited them in, locked the special eyeglasses on their heads, and led them to the palace. Along the way, he told everyone

that Dorothy had melted the Wicked Witch of the West. The people were so excited by the news that they forgot their fear of the Cowardly Lion and joined the growing crowd following Dorothy and her friends to the palace.

The same guard was on duty at the doors of the palace, and he let them in right away. Inside, the same green girl led them to their old rooms, so they could rest before meeting with Oz. The guard sent a message to Oz that the group had returned and that the Wicked Witch of the West was dead.

The friends expected to be seen right

away, but Oz didn't call them that day—or the next day, or even the day after that.

Yet another day passed, and they were still waiting impatiently to see Oz. The Scarecrow got so impatient that he went to the green girl and asked her to take another message to Oz. "Please tell him," said the Scarecrow, "that we have endured many hardships to fulfill his request. And now we have been kept waiting for days. Tell him that if he does not see us at once, we will call on the Winged Monkeys to take us before him!"

The Scarecrow's idea worked! Oz remembered how the Winged Monkeys had chased him out of the Wicked Witch's kingdom, and he didn't like them at all. He sent a message back to the friends: "You are to come to the throne room tomorrow morning," said the guard, "at four minutes after nine o'clock."

Promptly at 9:04 the next morning, the friends were shown into the throne room of Oz, the Great and Terrible. Dorothy expected to see the enormous, hairless head. The Scarecrow expected to see the beautiful fairy. The Tin Woodman expected to see the huge, shaggy beast, and the Cowardly Lion expected to see the immense ball of fire. The throne room looked exactly as each of them remembered, but there was no one on the throne. Oz was nowhere in sight.

Suddenly, a voice came thundering down from the ceiling. "I am Oz," it said, "the Great and Terrible. Why do you wish to see me?"

Quite startled, everyone looked all around, but still saw no one.

"Where are you?" asked Dorothy.

"I am everywhere, but I am invisible to your eyes," said the voice. "However, I will sit on my throne so you know which way to speak." The voice floated down as it talked, until it seemed to come from the gigantic throne. "Now tell me," it ordered. "Why did you demand to see me?"

"Surely you remember us," said Dorothy. "We have come to claim our promises from you, Great Oz."

"What promises?" asked the voice.

What? Oz, the Great and Terrible, did not remember his promises? This upset the friends so much that they all started talking at once.

"You promised to send Toto and me back to our home in Kansas if I killed the Wicked Witch of the West for you!" exclaimed Dorothy.

"You promised to give me brains!" said the Scarecrow.

"You promised to give me a heart!" said the Tin Woodman.

"You promised to give me some courage!" said the Cowardly Lion.

"Is the Wicked Witch of the West really dead?" asked the voice.

Dorothy thought that the voice trembled a bit. "Yes, I melted her," she said, sadly. "I didn't mean to, but I did. Now she's gone forever."

"Dear me!" the voice said. "This is quite sudden. Come back to me tomorrow; I need time to think about this."

"You've had plenty of time already," said the Tin Woodman angrily.

"We won't wait another day!" exclaimed the Scarecrow.

"You promised!" chimed in Dorothy.

The Cowardly Lion, however, thought that it would be best to scare the wizard, so he gave the biggest, loudest roar he possibly could. It was so big and loud—and sudden—that it frightened poor Toto. In his fear, the little dog leaped away from the Cowardly Lion and accidentally knocked over a tall screen that stood in the corner of the throne room. As it fell over with a crash, Dorothy and her friends stared with wonder. There, behind the fallen screen, was a little, old man with a bald head and a very wrinkled face. The little, old man seemed just as surprised as they were.

The Tin Woodman rushed over with his axe held high. He was ready to fight if any danger seemed to threaten his friends. "Who are you?" demanded the Tin Woodman.

"Why, I am Oz, the Great and Terrible," the little, old man said in a quavery voice. "Please don't hurt me. I will do anything that you ask."

The friends all stared at him in surprise and dismay. "Oz?" said Dorothy. "You can't be! Oz is an enormous head!"

"Oz is a beautiful fairy!" exclaimed the Scarecrow.

"Oz is a huge, shaggy beast!" cried the Tin Woodman.

"Oz is an immense ball of fire," growled the Cowardly Lion.

"You're all wrong, I'm afraid," said the little, old man. "Oz is just an ordinary person—just me, making believe."

"Making believe?" said Dorothy. "You mean that you aren't a great wizard?"

"No, I'm not. I'm just—"

"You're just a faker! A humbug!" said the Scarecrow in a woeful voice.

"Well, yes," said the little, old man, beginning to sound almost pleased with himself. "I am a humbug. But my subjects don't know that. I arrived here in such an unusual way, they all thought that I must have great powers," he explained. "So I just let them think that I was a great and terrible wizard. But I'm really a fellow from Omaha, Nebraska—not far from where *you* come from, Dorothy."

"Not a wizard?" yelled the friends at the same time.

"What about the promises you made?" asked the Scarecrow.

"Shhh! They'll hear you, and I'll be ruined!" whispered Oz in a panicky voice. "They would never trust me again."

"This is terrible!" wailed the Tin Woodman. "How will I ever get a heart now?"

"Or my brains?" asked the Scarecrow.

"Or my courage?" asked the Cowardly Lion.

"And how will I ever get back to Kansas?" asked Dorothy. "Oh, dear, I'll never see Aunt Em or Uncle Henry again!"

"Oh, please don't fuss so!" cried Oz. "If my subjects hear any of this, I'll be in terrible trouble. I *knew* that I should never have let you in here the first time! I don't even let my subjects into the throne room, for fear that they might find out the truth. But I was so very bored, and so positive that you would go away and never come back that I let you come inside. And now you know the truth. Please keep my secret! If my subjects find out, I am sure that they will never forgive me!"

"How did you get here?" asked Dorothy. "Maybe we could go back the same way."

"I'm afraid not, my dear," said the old man, a little sadly. "You see, I used to work for a circus. As the circus traveled from place to place, I would go up in a hot-air balloon to advertise that the circus was in town. One day, the ropes that kept the balloon in place came loose. I floated higher and higher until a mighty wind blew up and swept me along for days and days. Then, one day, the balloon came to rest in this lovely land. The people thought that I was a great wizard

because of the way I arrived, so I stayed and built this city."

Here Oz paused to take a deep breath and look around at his spellbound audience. "I'll tell you another secret," he whispered. "The Emerald City isn't even really green. I just make my subjects wear green-tinted glasses so everything *looks* green. They have worn them for so long now, they have come to believe that it truly *is* an Emerald City. It makes them happy to think that they live in a beautiful, bejeweled place that is protected by a powerful wizard."

"But don't they remember what the place looked like when they built it?" Dorothy asked.

"Oh, no," said Oz. "You see, I was a very young man when I came here, and now I am very, very old. Things have been this way for so long, everyone has forgotten the time before I arrived."

"Why did you send us after the Wicked Witch of the West?" asked the Scarecrow.

"I have always been afraid of all the witches," Oz said. "I knew that there were four of them, with great powers, while there was just one of me, with no powers at all. I knew that the Good Witches of the North and South would never harm me, even if they found out the truth. But the Wicked Witches of the East and West—they were another story. Long ago, before I had this great city to protect me, the Wicked Witch of the West set her Winged Monkeys on me. The only reason the wicked witches never attacked me again is that this city is so grand and beautiful, they thought that my powers must be greater than theirs. They didn't dare to come here."

Oz sighed. "One day," he said with a glance at Dorothy, "I heard that your house had landed on the Wicked Witch of the East and killed her. Then you came here, wearing those silver shoes and with the mark of the Good Witch of the North on your forehead. I decided that I should

promise you anything, if it would make you go out and kill the only wicked witch left."

"You should be ashamed of yourself," Dorothy scolded.

"I am," said Oz.

"You were our only hope!" said the disappointed girl. "I think that you are a very bad man."

"Oh, no, my dear," said Oz quite gently. "I'm really a very *good* man; I'm just a very bad wizard."

"Does this mean that you can't give me brains?" asked the Scarecrow.

"You don't really need any," said Oz. "You never did. A brain does not make you wise—only experience can do that. When you met Dorothy, you were a brand-new scarecrow. Like any baby starting out in the world, you learned a little more every day. You are just like any other man—except, of course, that you are stuffed. The longer you are on earth, the more experience you will get and the more you will know."

"That may be true," said the Scarecrow, "but a promise is a promise. You should keep yours."

"Very well," sighed Oz. "Come tomorrow and I will give you brains, but I can't tell you how to use them. That, you must learn on your own."

"Oh, thank you!" cried the Scarecrow in great delight.

"What about my courage?" asked the Cowardly Lion in an anxious voice.

"You have plenty of that already," said Oz. "I have seen it myself. All you need is confidence in yourself. There is no living thing on this earth that doesn't feel fear when it faces danger. True courage is in standing up to your fears, and you have plenty of that kind of courage already."

"Maybe so," said the Cowardly Lion doubtfully, "but I won't be happy until I have the kind of courage that makes you *forget* that you're afraid."

"Oh, all right," said Oz. "I'll give you that kind of courage tomorrow."

"What about my heart?" asked the Tin Woodman.

"If you ask me," said Oz, "you're better off without one. Having a heart makes most people unhappy, because sooner or later, it gets broken, which hurts more than you can imagine. You don't really need a heart. You don't know how lucky you are!"

"*You* may think so," argued the Tin Woodman, "but I don't. I will bear every heartache without a fuss, if you will only give me the heart you promised me."

"Very well, come tomorrow and you shall get one," Oz told him.

"What about Toto and me?" said Dorothy eagerly. "Will you send us back to Kansas tomorrow?"

"That, I'm afraid, I have no idea how to do," Oz told her. Seeing Dorothy's eyes begin to fill with tears, he rushed on. "Just give me a few days, and I'll try to come up with a way to get over the desert. Until then, you will all be my guests here in the palace. But you must promise not to tell my secret to anyone."

They agreed and went back to their rooms. They were all looking forward to the next day. Even Dorothy began to feel a little hopeful that "the Great and Terrible Faker," as she called him, would somehow figure out a way to get her back to Kansas.

Chapter 19
The Rewards

The following morning, the Scarecrow could hardly contain his excitement. "The next time you see me," he told his friends before going into the throne room, "I'll be just like other men!"

"I always liked you as you were," said Dorothy, very quietly.

"You're very kind," he said, "but you'll think even more of me once you hear all the great ideas my new brain is going to come up with!" With that, he stepped forward and knocked on the throne room door.

"Come in," said Oz.

"I'm here to get my brain," said the Scarecrow, stepping forward. He was still eager, but a little nervous, too. After all, it wasn't often that a person got magic performed on him.

Oz asked him to sit down. "I hope you don't mind," the old man told the Scarecrow, "but I will have to take your head off for a little while, so I can put your brain in the proper place."

"Oh, it's quite all right, as long as my head is better when you put it back on than when you took it off," the Scarecrow replied.

Oz took off the Scarecrow's head and took it to a back room. The room was crowded with shelves holding all sorts of bottles and bags and various odd things. There was the big head that Dorothy had talked to, and the fairy costume the Scarecrow had seen. Other costumes were there as well.

First, Oz pulled all the straw out of the Scarecrow's head. Next, he took some

bran from one jar and a bunch of pins and needles from another jar and mixed them all together. Then he opened the Scarecrow's head and poured the mixture in. Finally, he stuffed straw in around it, to hold everything in place, and closed the head up again.

"There we are," said Oz, putting the head back on the Scarecrow's body. "All done. You now have a, er, um, 'bran-new' brain! A rather large one, I might add."

Slowly, the Scarecrow stood up. He felt his head and began to smile. It felt much larger and heavier than before. Oz had given him brains!

Happily, he thanked Oz and ran out to tell his friends, who were waiting patiently outside the door. They all stared at his head, which was absolutely bulging with his new brains.

"How do you feel?" asked Dorothy.

"Great!" he boasted. "I feel very wise."

"Why do you have pins and needles sticking out of your head?" asked the Tin Woodman curiously.

"To show how sharp he is, of course!" said the Cowardly Lion.

"Oh, that makes sense," said the Tin Woodman. "Well, now it's time for me to go get my heart. Wish me luck." With those words and a wave, he stepped forward and knocked on the throne room door.

"Come in," said Oz.

"I'm here to get my heart," said the Tin Woodman, stepping forward.

"All right," said Oz, "but I'll have to cut

your chest open, so I can put your heart in the right place. I hope it won't hurt."

"Even if it did, I wouldn't mind, just so long as I got a heart in the bargain," said the Tin Woodman.

So Oz took out some very sharp shears and cut a hole in the Tin Woodman's chest. Then he opened a small box and took out a pink, silk heart stuffed with sawdust. "How do you like it?" he asked the Tin Woodman.

"Oh, it's beautiful!" said the Tin Woodman joyously. "Is it a *good* heart? Will it make me gentle and kind?"

"Yes, of course," said Oz, putting the

heart inside the Tin Woodman's chest. He replaced the square of tin and then welded it back into place. "I'm sorry about the patch," he told the Tin Woodman, "but it couldn't be helped."

"That's perfectly all right," cried the Tin Woodman. He was so happy that he gave Oz a big hug, which made Oz laugh. Then the Tin Woodman dashed out to tell his friends about his beautiful new heart.

They congratulated him and admired his heart, which they could hear bouncing around in his chest. This inspired the Cowardly Lion so much that he almost forgot to be afraid when it was his turn to knock on the throne room door.

"Come in," said Oz.

"I—I—I have come for my c-courage," he stuttered, stepping forward.

"All right. Come on in," said Oz, waving the Lion into the little back room.

Oz studied the shelves a moment, then reached for a heavy, green bottle. He shook the bottle to stir up its contents,

then poured some of the liquid into a beautiful greenish-gold dish. "Here," he told the Cowardly Lion. "Drink this."

The Lion sniffed suspiciously at the dish. "What is it?" he wanted to know.

"I don't know what to call it when it's in a bottle or a dish," said Oz. "But once it's inside of you, it will be courage. That is the only way courage can work," he explained. "It has to be inside you."

"Oh, well, that certainly makes sense," said the Cowardly Lion, and apologized for hesitating. Then, without another thought, he drank every drop in the dish.

Oz studied the creature's face. "How do you feel now?" he asked.

"Full of courage! Thank you, Oz!" the Lion roared, then ran out to celebrate with his friends.

Alone once again, Oz smiled to himself. "Well, I made those fellows happy. I guess I'm not such a big faker, after all!" Then he remembered Dorothy. He sat down and propped his chin on his hands. He still had no idea how to get her home. This was going to require serious thought.

Chapter 20

The Hot-air Balloon

For three days, Dorothy wandered sadly about the palace. She had heard not even a peep from Oz, and was beginning to despair of seeing her home ever again. Her friends were all happy, though, because each had had his fondest wish come true.

The Scarecrow was delighted with all the great thoughts he was thinking, but he wouldn't tell anyone what they were because he didn't think they would understand them. The Tin Woodman was thrilled with the way it felt to have a heart thumping about in his chest, and declared that he was ever so much kinder to people and felt every joy and pain so much more deeply. As for the Lion—cowardly no longer—he told everyone that he feared nothing at all anymore, not even a horde of horrible Kalidahs.

At long last, on the fourth day, Oz sent for Dorothy. She ran to the throne room door at once and knocked.

"Come in," said Oz. "Have a seat."

"Do you know how to get Toto and me home to Kansas?" she asked hopefully.

"Well," said Oz, "out of this country, at any rate. We shall build another balloon. That is how I got here, so I don't see why we can't leave the same way."

"We? Are you going with me?"

"Why not?" said Oz. "I'm tired of being a humbug wizard, spending day after day hiding in my room so no one will learn my secret. I'd rather go to Kansas with you and find a circus to work for."

Dorothy was so excited that she ran to tell her friends, then ran back to help Oz make the balloon. They cut out long strips of green silk, then stitched them together. In three days, they had made a great, big bag out of the material. Oz turned it inside out and painted the inside with glue, to make it airtight. "Now," he said, "all we need is something to ride in!"

Oz dug out the biggest laundry basket he could find, then tied it to the narrow end of the big green bag. "There!" he declared at last. "Our balloon awaits!"

Oz sent word to the people of the Emerald City, telling them that he would be going on a long journey beyond the clouds, to visit a fellow wizard.

On the day of the trip, everyone in the city came to see them off. The Tin Woodman brought over a pile of wood that he cut to set on fire. Oz brought out the balloon and held it over the fire so it filled with air. Then he attached it to the basket and the basket rose from the ground.

Oz climbed into the basket, waved to his people, and made a little speech. "While I am gone," he told them, "the Scarecrow will rule over you. You must obey him as you would me. Have no fear. He is a very wise man."

Oz looked around for Dorothy. "Come, Dorothy," he called. "Hurry, girl, or the balloon will fly away without you!"

"But I can't find Toto anywhere!" She was running here and there, looking for her little dog. "I can't leave him!"

Toto had dashed into the crowd, chas-

ing after a kitten. Dorothy heard him barking and ran to catch him, then ran as fast as she could back to the balloon.

Just as she got to the balloon and stretched out her hand to grab Oz's, there was a sudden cracking sound and the ropes anchoring the balloon to the ground broke free. Oz tried again to grab her hand, but he couldn't—the balloon was rising too fast. Dorothy was out of his reach.

"Come back. Please!" she screamed. "Oh, please come back! I want to go, too!"

"I can't stop now," shouted Oz. "I don't know how! I'm sorry. Good-bye, Dorothy! Good-bye, all!" His voice was getting ever more faint, until it disappeared altogether. Then the balloon disappeared into the clouds.

Chapter 21

News of Another Witch

Dorothy sat down and sobbed. Now what was she going to do? The Lion, the Tin Woodman, and the Scarecrow tried to comfort her, but all she could do was go back to her room.

The next morning, the friends gathered in the throne room. The Scarecrow was in charge now, so he sat on the gigantic throne.

"Don't worry, Dorothy. We'll get you home somehow," he told her. "Let's think."

They all thought, but the Scarecrow must have been thinking the hardest—pins and needles were already sticking out of his head. Suddenly, he jumped up and shouted, "I have it! Why don't you use the Golden Cap again, and ask the Winged Monkeys to take you home?"

"That's a wonderful idea!" Dorothy exclaimed smiling. "Why didn't I think of it before?" She ran to her room to get the Golden Cap, then hurried back to the throne room.

When she returned, she popped it on

her head and followed the instructions. In an instant the Winged Monkeys appeared, and their leader flew over and landed in front of Dorothy.

"Hail," he told her, bowing. "What is your second command?"

"To go home," she told him. "Please carry me over the desert to Kansas."

The leader of the Winged Monkeys shook his head. "I'm sorry," he said, "but we can't do that. We can do many things in our own country, but we cannot leave here. We couldn't make it over the desert." He said good-bye and flew away, with his followers flapping and chattering behind him.

"Now what?" sniffed Dorothy, fighting to hold back tears. "I just wasted the Golden Cap's powers by making a wish that the Winged Monkeys cannot grant me."

The Scarecrow had been thinking again, and was ready for her question. "Let's ask the soldier with the green whiskers," he said. "Maybe he knows what you can do." He called out the soldier's name, and the man stepped timidly into the room.

"Come in, please," said the Scarecrow. "We have a question for you."

So the soldier came closer, looking around with great curiosity. Oz had never allowed him to enter the throne room.

"Have you any idea how this girl and her dog can cross the desert and get back to Kansas?" the Scarecrow asked him.

"No, I don't," was his answer. "No one ever crossed the desert before, except the Great Oz."

Dorothy's hopes were dashed again. "Is there no one else who can help me?"

"Well," said the soldier, feeling sorry for the girl, "you could go to Glinda, the Witch of the South. She is the most powerful of all the witches. She rules over the Quadlings, the people of the lands to the South, and she lives in a castle right on the edge of the desert. Perhaps she can help you."

"Is Glinda a good witch?" Dorothy wanted to know.

"Oh, yes, very good!" said the soldier. "The Quadlings say that she is kind to everyone. Just follow the road straight to the South and you will reach her castle. You can't miss it! But take care—you must go through thick woods, and you will see wild beasts and all sorts of dangerous things. That is why Quadlings hardly ever visit our city, or we theirs."

Dangerous or not, Dorothy decided, she had to go see Glinda, the Good Witch of the South.

Dangerous or not, her friends decided to go with her.

Chapter 22

Strange People and Places

They left the next morning at dawn. The soldier with the green whiskers brought them to the Guardian of the Gates, who took off their glasses and bade the Scarecrow to come back as soon as possible. He was their ruler now, after all. The Scarecrow assured the Guardian that he would return soon and, once again, the little band of friends started a journey together. Full of hope that Dorothy would have success this time, they walked all day long, laughing and talking.

That night, they slept in a field of bright green grass and colorful flowers. Early the next morning, they took to the road again. Eventually, they came to a vast forest. It was tangled and thick and went on as far as they could see in every direction. The trees were so close together that they couldn't find any openings between trunks and branches.

Then the Scarecrow spied a gap that looked as if it might be big enough for them all to squeeze through. So he stepped forward. But the moment his foot touched the ground under the opening, tree branches whipped into motion and twisted themselves around him. They picked him up, twirled him around a few times, then tossed him to the ground, right at the feet of his startled friends. He wasn't a bit hurt, just a little dizzy and very surprised.

"That tree picked you up and threw you out of the forest," said the Tin Woodman.

"I know," the Scarecrow said.

Just then, the Lion spotted another gap in the woods. "Let me try it," said the Scarecrow. "If they do it again, it won't hurt me the way it would any of you."

He stepped into the new gap—a little more cautiously this time—but once again the tree picked him up, twirled him around a few times, then tossed him to the ground.

"How strange!" said Dorothy.

"Yes," the Lion agreed. "These trees don't seem to want us to get through."

"Let me try," said the Tin Woodman. He walked forward with his axe held ready, and when a branch swooped down to grab him, he swung his axe and chopped the branch in half. The tree began to shake, as if it was unhappy or in pain, but it didn't grab at him again.

"Come on, everyone. Run through quickly," called the Tin Woodman.

So they did, and made it safely inside the forest. Once inside, there was plenty of room to walk, and none of the other trees tried to attack them.

The group walked on until they came, abruptly, to the edge of the forest. There, right in front of them, was a wall that looked as smooth as glass. In fact, it seemed to be made of white china, just like fine dinner plates. The wall was rather tall, and so wide that it seemed without end. The friends didn't dare try to go around it for fear of losing sight of the road. They had no choice but to climb over it.

The Tin Woodman went back to the forest and began cutting up an old, fallen tree to build a ladder. He dragged the ladder to the wall and propped the ladder against it. All four of them climbed over, one by one, with the Scarecrow going first. As they reached the top of the wall and looked over, each one gasped in surprise and said, "My goodness!"

On the other side of the wall was a country made entirely of china. There were little china houses no taller than Dorothy's waist, and little china barns and fences. Behind the fences were little china cows and sheep and horses and chickens. There were little china cats and dogs and birds. Even the people were made of china and wore brightly colored clothes.

None of the china people or animals paid any attention to Dorothy and her friends, so they jumped off the wall and started to walk through the china country as carefully as they could. A little, china princess dressed all in red walked in front of them. The princess was so pretty that Dorothy wanted to take her home to Aunt Em, so she ran after the little doll.

"Please don't chase me," cried the china princess in a fearful voice. "I may fall and be cracked."

"I'm sorry," Dorothy said. "I just wanted to take you home for my Aunt Em."

"I would be very unhappy there," said the princess. "Here, I can walk and talk. But if I leave this country, my joints will go stiff, and I won't be able to move or talk anymore. It would be very boring."

"I had no idea!" said Dorothy. "I don't want you to be unhappy. We'll be very careful not to crack anyone as we walk through here."

It took them another two hours to get to the other end of the china country. They had walked very carefully and hadn't broken anything, but they were tired. It was hard to be so careful all the time!

They came to another wall, this one low enough to climb over without a ladder.

The land on the other side of the wall was not easy to travel through. First they had to cross a swampy, muddy area. Then they had to travel through another dark forest, with wild animals howling all around them. They made it through safely, however, then walked on until they came to a tall, rocky hill.

They rested a moment, trying to figure out the best way to climb it, when an angry voice came from behind the rocks, saying, "You cannot cross this hill. Go back now."

"Why not?" asked the Scarecrow.

"Because it's ours," said the voice, which came from an odd-looking man who was coming toward them from behind the rock. He was short and wide, with a flat head, like a hammer, and no arms.

The Scarecrow apologized to the man, but told him that they *had* to cross it, to get to the land of the Quadlings. The Scarecrow stepped forward. In the blink of an eye, the man's neck stretched like a lightning-fast snake, propelling his head right at the Scarecrow. The flat top of his head hit the Scarecrow so hard that he rolled all the way back to the bottom of the hill. As the Scarecrow's friends hurried down to see if he was all right, the man's neck snapped back into place.

Then from all over the hillside, they

heard peals of laughter. They looked up to see a hammer-head creature peeking over or around every rock on the hill. There were hundreds of them!

This made the Lion angry, so he roared and charged at another rock. He got the same treatment—and more laughter.

"There is no way we can get past them," groaned the aching Lion.

The Tin Woodman agreed. "I think you should put on your Golden Cap," he told Dorothy, "and use your last wish to have the Winged Monkeys carry us over this hill. Not even I can stand up to a bunch of hammer-heads!"

Dorothy agreed, and put on her cap. When she said the charm, the Winged Monkeys arrived with their usual noise.

"This is the last time you can use our services," the leader told her, after bowing low in greeting. "What do you wish?"

"Please carry us over this hill, past the hammer-heads, and into the land of the Quadlings," Dorothy requested.

Right away, the Winged Monkeys did as they were asked. They set Dorothy and her friends down in a wonderful place. It looked like other lands they had traveled through, except here everything was red, instead of the blue favored by the Munchkins or the yellow of the Winkies.

In the distance, they saw a glorious castle. When they reached it, they were met by three guards—each was a girl dressed in a red uniform—who let them into the castle at once.

Chapter 23

The Red Castle

The guards led the travelers to rooms where they could freshen up. Dorothy washed her face and brushed her hair. The Lion swept dust from his mane and tail, the Scarecrow patted himself tidy, and the Tin Woodman oiled his joints.

Then the guards led them down a hallway to a big room. At the far end was a huge throne that glittered with bright red rubies. Seated on the throne was the most beautiful person they had ever seen. She had a youthful, smiling face

and long, wavy red hair that fell below the shoulders of her snow-white gown. Her eyes, which were a clear, sky blue, seemed to hold all the wisdom and kindness in the world. It was Glinda, the Good Witch of the South.

Dorothy had a hard time believing that someone so young and beautiful could be a witch. All the witches she had ever seen had been very old; the evil ones had been ugly, besides. Even the Good Witch of the North had been ancient and wrinkled. It was very hard not to stare.

"What can I do for you, my dear?" Glinda asked in a soft, pleasant voice.

Dorothy told her the whole story, then said, "I have come all this way to ask if you know a way for Toto and me to get back home to Kansas. You are our last hope."

"I do know a way," Glinda replied. "I will help you, but you must give me the Golden Cap in return."

"Of course I will! For me, it would only be a pretty thing to wear, as I have used up my wishes," said the girl. "You get only three, you know," she added.

"Yes, I know," said Glinda with a laugh. "I know just how to use my three wishes, too. Now," she said, turning to Dorothy's three friends. "What are you going to do after Dorothy goes home?"

"I will return to the Emerald City and use my brains to rule wisely, just as Oz wished," said the Scarecrow, proudly.

"Very well," said Glinda. "I shall use one of my wishes to have the Winged Monkeys carry you back to the Emerald City. And you?" she asked the Tin Woodman.

"The Winkies asked me to be their ruler after we killed the Wicked Witch of the West and freed them from slavery," he said. "So I shall return there and use my heart to rule over them as kindly and gently as I can."

"Then I shall use my second wish to have the Winged Monkeys carry you back to the land of the Winkies." said Glinda. "Lion, what about you?"

"I want to return to my home in the forest and show all the animals how brave I've become. With my courage, I am now truly the King of the Beasts," the Lion said.

"In that case," said the Good Witch, "I shall use my third wish to have you carried back to your forest." Glinda now turned back to Dorothy. "May I have the Golden Cap now?"

Dorothy took out the Golden Cap and handed it over to Glinda, who gave her a hug and a smile. "What will you do with the Cap after you have used up your three wishes?" Dorothy wondered.

"I shall give it back to the Winged Monkeys," said Glinda kindly. "They can rule over themselves at last. For far too long, they have been slaves to whoever owns the Golden Cap, and they most certainly do not need to have it fall into the hands of someone like the Wicked Witch of the West. They deserve their freedom."

The Scarecrow, Tin Woodman, and Lion all thanked Glinda for her generosity. She was a very good witch, indeed, they thought. Dorothy thought the same thing, but couldn't help but speak up.

"If you please," said the girl, "may I ask how *I* am to get home?"

"Why, Dorothy," Glinda said, "you have had the power to go home to your Aunt Em and Uncle Henry since the very first day that you arrived here. You can command your silver shoes to take you anywhere you wish to go."

"I'm glad that you didn't go home right away," said the Scarecrow. "If you had, I never would have gotten my brains."

"And I never would have gotten my heart," said the Tin Woodman.

"And I never would have gotten my courage," said the Lion.

"I'm rather glad that I didn't know about the power of the silver shoes," said Dorothy. "If I had known, I would have gone home immediately, and I never would have met such wonderful friends or had such amazing adventures. I am glad that each one of you finally got what he most wanted in the world."

Dorothy looked around at the smiling-but-sad faces of her dear friends. "I will miss all of you terribly," she said, "but now I have to go home to Aunt Em and Uncle Henry. They must be so worried about me!" She picked up Toto, who was trying to run away again, and held him tightly in her arms. Dorothy turned to Glinda, the Good Witch of the South. "I am ready now," she said. "How do I ask my silver shoes to take me home?"

"You simply click your heels together three times and tell the shoes where you want to go. In three steps, they will take you to Kansas—or anywhere else in the world you might wish to go."

"That's it?" Dorothy exclaimed. "But it is so easy."

"I know, but that is the way it is done," Glinda assured her.

So Dorothy and each of her friends exchanged a kiss and hug, and they tearfully waved their good-byes. The Tin Woodman cried so hard that the Scarecrow had to oil his jaw to keep it from rusting! Then, concentrating very hard on her home in Kansas, Dorothy clicked her heels together three times and said, "Take me to my home in Kansas, please." She was a polite girl, after all.

Suddenly, she was flying through the

air. The wind was whipping through her hair, and her clothes flapped about so hard that they almost hurt. She held on to Toto as tightly as she could, but now he was being very good and didn't wiggle at all. Finally, Dorothy landed on a patch of gray grass. She didn't land hard, but she had been going so fast that she rolled over several times before she stopped.

As soon as she stopped rolling, she sat up and looked around. She was in Kansas! "I'm home!" she yelled joyously.

She ran toward the new farmhouse—the old one got blown away in the cyclone, if you remember. "Aunt Em, Uncle Henry, I'm home!" she called out. "Toto, too. We have had the most wonderful adventures!"

Just then, Dorothy looked down and realized that the silver shoes were not on her feet anymore. They had fallen off during her whirlwind trip home, and were lost forever. But she soon forgot all about them, because she was home at last.

Aunt Em and Uncle Henry came running out of the farmhouse and gathered Dorothy into their arms while Toto barked and jumped around at their feet. They were so happy to see her. It had been even more gray and miserable without Dorothy around. Now that she was home, everything was brighter. Things were good again.

The End

ABOUT THE AUTHOR

L. Frank Baum was born in Chittenango, New York, on May 15, 1856. Interested in writing from an early age, he chose among his many pursuits journalism as a career. Baum worked as a newspaper editor in Aberdeen, South Dakota, and Chicago, Illinois. He also worked as an actor, playwright, salesman, and magazine editor.

Baum became interested in writing fiction for children as well and, in 1897, he published *Mother Goose in Prose*, his first children's book. *The Wonderful Wizard of Oz* was published in 1900. It was so popular that subsequently he wrote 13 more Oz titles. Baum wrote many other books as well, but none was ever as well-known or loved as the original Oz story.

L. Frank Baum died in Hollywood, California, on May 6, 1919.

Treasury of Illustrated Classics™

Adventures of Huckleberry Finn
The Adventures of Robin Hood
The Adventures of Sherlock Holmes
The Adventures of Tom Sawyer
Alice in Wonderland
Anne of Green Gables
Black Beauty
The Call of the Wild
Gulliver's Travels
Heidi
Jane Eyre
The Legend of Sleepy Hollow
& Rip Van Winkle
A Little Princess
Little Women
Moby Dick
Oliver Twist
Peter Pan
Rebecca of Sunnybrook Farm
Robinson Crusoe
The Secret Garden
Swiss Family Robinson
Treasure Island
20,000 Leagues Under the Sea
The Wizard of Oz